THE DEAD LIFTERS

DEVESH PANDEY

Made with ❤ on the Notion Press Platform
www.notionpress.com

This decribes the haunts that a cementry worker may feel at night in cementry

Contents

Foreword

Acknowledgements

*Stating the fictional story about the dead lifters and their
community
and the worker that works in cementry that how
haunting and mysterious the night at cementry
can be....*

1
The introduction

you probably wondering who i am, so let me tell you

Hello this is **_Avinash._**

Yes I am the one who expirenced the abnormal things at the cementry. I told many people about and none of them belived it now its my turnd to make them belive that this is true.

cementry

2
The Dead Lifters

It was the rainy day and also my first day at the cementry waiting for the the instructions to be given to me after the dead body entered the cementry as I mentioned the night was way to dark and in addition the night was rainy too my head staff told me

> "*get down real quick recive the body in the room before they see it*"

i said **AFFERMATIVE** without listening to the command completly.

I took the body and kept it in the the freezer inside the room. I told my head that the work is done but we can't do **"antim sanskar"** this night because it was heavily raining so my head worker told me to stay with the body till morning i agreed with that because it was my first day. I was sitting at the chair trying to sleep but when i closed my eyes i thinked about the statement that was told to me when i was reciving the dead body. He told **"*recive the body before they see it*"** who are they, who will see the body.

I was proceeding to sleep then suddenly i heard a knocking sound at the door I opend the eyes and saw there was bunch of people standing at the door asking about the details of the dead body. I thought they were the family members.They proceed to check the diary

they said in the *deep voice* "**Where is the dead body from**" i said "**I don't know**"

i asked " **Who are you? why are you asking all this?** " He ignores all the people at the room to take the body. I said " **why you doing! it who are you?** "

he said in *harsh voice*

" *it should not bother you otherwise you too will face this oneday*"

There face was hid with a mask and they were holding weapons.

I started to question them but one of them hit my head with the rod he was holding ....

Later........

I woke up in the hospital my head was paining a lot. The docter told me my head got 16 stiches i was wondering what happend that night, lately my senior came to me asking what happened to **'body'** i told some group of people came to the room and was asking about the body. i thought they were his family members but they were not

My senior told me : - **No worries take rest and sleep will talk after you join the duty**

I responded : **ok sir**

Later i was discharged from hospital and went to my house my mother was waiting for me

She told:- **where were you son? and what happened to you**

I said:- **nothing just an small acciden**t

I told :- **Maa i am very hungary can i get something to eat.**

She said:- **yes son ! sit i will bring the food**

Lately, I went to sleep,

I woke up and asked to join the duty later i joined the duty. Touched my mother feets and went to duty. My senior told me "How are you now?" i replied " **Fine sir**" Later another dead body came to cementry I recived the body noted to the dairy and took the body to proceed the **'anitim sanskar'** I did all the rituals with the priest and the his family members i went to my compartment just to take a little rest they day was very hectic i told to my colleague he said yes but soon you will get use to it *a lil laugh*. we proceed to take the dinner, after having the dinner we went for a walk we were just walking and chatting to each other. suddenly i thought to ask him about the incident happened with me i asked to "Santosh". you know what happened with me he responded "no". I told the whole incident, he replied *shivering* **I.....I..I don't know.** I said what happend why are you shivering, He said 'nothing' I took him to the compartment and told please explain me what happend with me.

He said really Brother "i don't know ". I know he was hiding something form me. i also told him its fine you take rest....

It was 10:00 PM. i was thinking to take a round of cementry i went for the round I took my torch and went for the walk and saw the same group of the people around the banyan tree they were performing some rituals I went close to see whats happening but my head staff stopped me........

TO BE CONTINUED IN NEXT PART